W9-BIX-830

The Night Dragon

In memory of my granny, Gytha,
who filled my world with strength and color.

Brimming with creative inspiration, how-to projects, and useful information to enrich your everyday life, Quarto Knows is a favorite destination for those pursuing their interests and passions. Visit our site and dig deeper with our books into your area of interest: Quarto Creates, Quarto Cooks, Quarto Homes, Quarto Lives, Quarto Drives, Quarto Explores, Quarto Gifts, or Quarto Kids.

The Night Dragon © 2018 Quarto Publishing plc. Text © 2018 Naomi Howarth.
Illustrations © 2018 Naomi Howarth.

First published in 2018 by Lincoln Children's Books,
an imprint of The Quarto Group.
400 First Avenue North, Suite 400, Minneapolis, MN 55401, USA.
T (612) 344-8100 F (612) 344-8692 **www.QuartoKnows.com**

The right of Naomi Howarth to be identified as the author and illustrator of this work has been asserted by her in accordance with the Copyright, Designs and Patents Act, 1988 (United Kingdom).

All rights reserved.

No part of this publication may be reproduced, stored in a retrieval system, or transmitted, in any form, or by any means, electrical, mechanical, photocopying, recording, or otherwise without the prior written permission of the publisher or a license permitting restricted copying.

A catalogue record for this book is available from the British Library.

ISBN 978-1-78603-107-5

The illustrations were created in watercolor
Set in Cormorant Infant

Published by Rachel Williams
Designed by Karissa Santos
Edited by Katie Cotton
Production by Jenny Cundill and Kate O'Riordan

Manufactured in Shenzhen, China RD042018

9 8 7 6 5 4 3 2 1

The Night Dragon

Naomi Howarth

Lincoln
Children's Books

On top of a very high mountain, in a land far away, lived a dragon.

Her name was Maud.
Maud was one of five dragons,
but she wasn't like the others at all.
They were night dragons.

Every evening, when the sun was low in the sky, Delbert, Gar, Brimlad, and Nelda would wake up from a long sleep. They would swoop into the air, breathing huge flames of fire, and fill the sky with great gray, sooty clouds. As these clouds covered the sun, darkness would fall and day would turn to night.

But Maud didn't fly,

breathe fire,

or cast great gray, sooty clouds over the land.

"Why don't you fly, Maud?"
snarled Delbert.

"She's a weedy wimp!
Her wings are too weak," croaked Gar.

"She's not tough enough to take on the sun!" shouted Brimlad.

"It's best if she doesn't bother, the pretty little thing!" cackled Nelda.

"It must be true," thought Maud. "I'll never be a night dragon."

Maud's only friend was Mouse.
"I wish I could fly, and breathe fire, and fill the sky with great gray, sooty clouds," Maud would say.

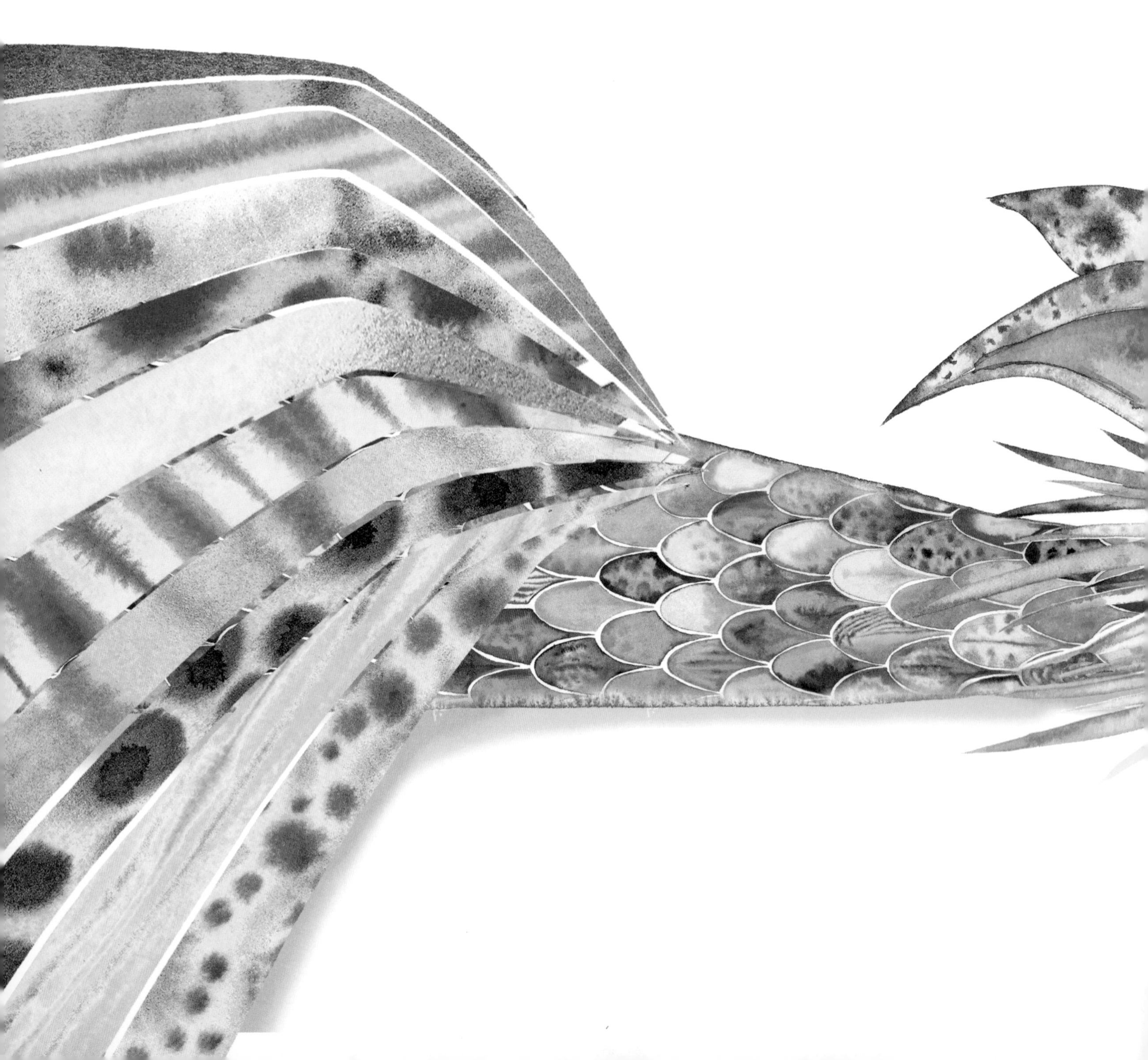

"But you could, Maud!" Mouse always squeaked. "Don't listen to the others! If you tried, you'd see that you can do those things just fine. You don't need to be a big, scary brute to be a night dragon. You just need to be yourself."

But Maud didn't quite believe him.

One afternoon, on the day of Brimlad's 557th birthday, he decided to throw a party. All the dragons were invited, except for Maud.

Maud watched as they ate,
drank, and fought until one by one, each
dragon fell into a deep, unshakeable sleep.

As the day drew on, the dragons still didn't wake up. Maud looked out over the land, but something was very different. The sky was completely empty! There were no clouds and nightfall was nowhere to be seen. Maud didn't know what to do.

"Maud," said Mouse, "you have to try and fly, otherwise the sky will stay light all night!"
"I can't!" whispered Maud. "I'm afraid to."
"I know you can do it, Maud," insisted Mouse.
"I will come with you, and we can fly together."

With Mouse's words in her ear,
Maud felt a little bit braver.
There was only one thing for it . . .

Maud stepped off the edge of the mountain
and began tumbling through the air.
"Use your wings, Maud!" squeaked Mouse.

Maud beat her wings as hard as she could and suddenly, the ground grew smaller.

She wasn't tumbling anymore.

She was soaring!

The sun was still shining brightly over the land as Maud took a deep breath and blew out huge plumes of fire and great clouds of smoke.

But these clouds weren't gray.

They were every color of the rainbow!

Together, Maud and Mouse sailed over mountains and fields.

They glided above winding rivers.

They soared over cities, until the whole sky

was filled with brilliant hues.

When Maud and Mouse stopped to rest, they watched as the sun sank behind clouds of color, and night began to fall.

"Thank you for believing in me, Mouse," said Maud.

"Thank you for the adventure," he squeaked. "I rather like being a flying mouse! And look how beautiful you have made everything, just by being yourself."

From that day on,
Maud and Mouse have journeyed
far and wide, filling the skies with color
and helping the sun to set. And though the
other dragons still try to cover everything in great
gray, sooty clouds, Maud and Mouse keep flying.

So next time you see a colorful sunset,
you'll know that Maud and Mouse aren't far away.

The end.